I DEDICATE this book to my
♥ dear husband, CHRIS. ♥
(You are welcome for this and our marital bliss.)

And our FOUR growing SONS
who all fill up our hearts,
we both love you so much (even with all the FARTS!)

To our new BABY GIRL,
♥ whom we haven't yet met, ♥
you are so very LOVED—but you don't know it yet.

And to all of the others
★ who've stood by my side, ★
you are all just the BEST, and that can't be denied.

♥, Katie

A Little Offbeat Publishing, LLC
www.ALittleOffbeat.com

Author, Illustrator and Designer: Katie Weaver

Text & Illustration Copyright © 2021 A Little Offbeat Publishing, LLC
First Edition
1 3 5 7 9 10 8 6 4 2

Library of Congress Control Number: 2020924619
ISBN 978-1-7362673-0-1 (Hardcover)

A Little Offbeat Publishing, LLC offers special discounts when purchasing in larger volumes for various purposes. For more information or to inquire, please visit our website: www.ALittleOffbeat.com

Printed in China

WHEN THE SKY ROARS

WRITTEN & ILLUSTRATED BY
KATIE WEAVER

What's that RUMBLE I hear
on this bright summer day?
And just why is the sky turning cloudy and gray?
I think back to the times this has happened before.
Then the sky opens up, and I hear a loud ROAR!

As the ROARING gets louder ... I scramble inside and race straight to my room— it's the best place to hide.

So, I dive into bed,
     pull the covers up high,
         and I shut my eyes tight
             as I quietly cry.

But the longer I lie here,
     the sadder I feel,
         'cuz these storms are so loud,
             and the ROARING is real!

I REMEMBER that time
while with Gramps at the park,
large gray clouds moved in fast,
and the sky became DARK.

I had been on the slide
but was too scared to stay,
so we hid underneath
till the STORM went away.

And then once,
at the field, I'd just hit a HOME RUN...
when the sky loudly ROARED, but the game wasn't done!
We were safely ahead... but the storm was a threat!
And I SHIVERED and SHOOK, as I started to SWEAT.

SO . . .
I crisscross my arms,
and I STOMP on the floor!
I just have to find out what would
make the sky ROAR!

With a few fat BALLOONS fastened onto my rear,

I am off to the clouds as I face my BIG FEAR.
Now, the higher I travel, the more the wind blows,
and these OODLES of raindrops are drenching my clothes.

With a WHOOSH and a FLIP,
the wind places me down
on the fluffiest cloud,
floating high above town.

And I know in my heart this just has to be it—

I'll find out what is ROARING
and get it to quit!

Oh, my goodness! What's that in the wide-open blue?

It's a ship that is filled
with a LOUD pirate crew!

A huge SHIP in the sky?
How on earth can this be?
I have never seen ships
anywhere but the sea!

But these pirates are special—
they're dancing BALLET!
They are twirling in circles
while sailing away!

Are the pirates the ones who are RUMBLING the sky?
No ... I DON'T think they are, so I'll wave them goodbye.

Look at that up ahead! It's a thick, smoky cloud . . .
I see FIRE TRUCKS, too—and their sirens are loud!

They are hooking up hoses to put out each FLAME.
They are NOISY, and yet, I don't think they're to blame.

I am looking for something
that makes a loud ROAR, so
I must keep on searching
these clouds a bit more.

As I roam on and on,
I see NOTHING but skies...
oh, but wait, now I see a
HUMONGOUS surprise!

It's a dinosaur mom,
who is clearly annoyed.
She's discovered her pie was
COMPLETELY
DESTROYED!

She is calling her kids, hoping they will confess.
Look at this! They've returned,
and they're both such a MESS!

The kid dinos are SLIMY and covered in GOO.

Now the PIE crime is solved ...
clearly, Mom always KNEW!

Yes, their mom is prepared.
This has happened before.
So, she spoons in some BERRIES
and WHIPS UP one more.

With each forkful of pie that the dino kids eat,
"This is GREAT!" they ROAR loudly
while STOMPING their feet!

Now, the dinos are kind, and they share
some with me.
"Oh, this pie tastes DELIGHTFUL!
I surely agree!"

So, I say my FAREWELLS—
it's the end of the day.
With the last slice of PIE,
I now head on my way.

From now on, every time
I begin to hear THUNDER,
I won't be afraid, and
I won't even wonder.

'Cuz when the sky ROARS,
I will now know just why—
there are dinos enjoying
their mom's scrumptious pie!

FOUR BERRY CRUMB PIE

Yield: One 9" Pie | Serves: One Medium-Sized Dinosaur | Prep Time: 25 minutes | Cook Time: 45 Minutes

INGREDIENTS

Pie crust for a 9" deep dish pan
2 cups fresh or frozen raspberries
2 cups fresh or frozen strawberries
2 cups fresh or frozen blueberries
2 cups fresh or frozen blackberries
3/4 cup granulated sugar
1 tablespoon lemon juice
4 tablespoons cornstarch
2 tablespoons butter

Crumb Topping:
1 cup brown sugar
1 cup all purpose flour
1/4 cup of butter (cold)

INSTRUCTIONS

1. Combine berries, sugar, and lemon juice in a large saucepan and simmer over low-medium heat for 5-10 minutes. Stir slowly and gently.
2. Spoon 1/3-1/2 cup of the berry juice from the saucepan into a bowl. Stir in the cornstarch until smooth. Add the cornstarch mixture back into the berries and simmer over low heat for 4-5 minutes, until the berry mixture thickens. Be gentle.
3. Stir in butter. Remove from heat and allow mixture to cool for 20-30 minutes.
4. Pour into unbaked pie shell.
5. Combine crumb topping ingredients using a fork, stand mixer, or food processor until crumbly.
6. Cover berry filling with crumb topping and bake at 375 degrees for about 45 minutes.
7. For best results, allow pie to cool completely before serving
8. ROAR when you eat it!

KATIE WEAVER

Author | Illustrator | Book Designer & Formatter | Wife | Mama

In Northern Virginia, you'll find a weird MOTHER
with SO many kids—and she'll soon have another!
This life with her husband is CRAZY, no question.
(Not crazy for real, that is just an expression.)
Her love for all CHILDREN began with her own,
So she WRITES, and she DRAWS for all children unknown.
For the first time *(forever)*, her kids think she's COOL,
Which is so SUPER SPECIAL— it's truly her fuel.
She has many achievements for which she is PROUD,
although WRITING THIS BOOK has her up on a cloud.
Katie hopes that you'll LOVE IT *(it took her forever)*,
but this was, for certain, her FAVORITE ENDEAVOR.
With QUESTIONS or COMMENTS you have for this gal,
send an email or message—she loves a NEW PAL.
This would make her so glad—make her HEART feel complete.
(But be warned, little one, she's A LITTLE OFFBEAT.)

www.ALittleOffbeat.com

Photo by
@HeadShotDC

ALL ILLUSTRATIONS
WERE CREATED
BY HAND (& WITH ♥)
USING PHOTOSHOP
& A DIGITAL WACOM
TABLET.